Strega Nona
and
Her Tomatoes

D0950885

How to say:
Signora: Seen-YOR-uh
Bambolona: BOM-boh-LO-nuh

Strega Nona
and
Her Tomatoes

Written and illustrated by
Tomie dePaola

Ready-to-Read

Simon Spotlight
New York   London   Toronto   Sydney   New Delhi

"Let me see if any of my vegetables are ripe," said Strega Nona.

"TOMATOES!"
she shouted.

"My basket is full,"
said Strega Nona.

"I promised to give
two dozen ripe tomatoes
to the sisters
of the convent."

"I will count how many
I have," she said.

"Ten, eleven, twelve . . ."

"... twenty-four."

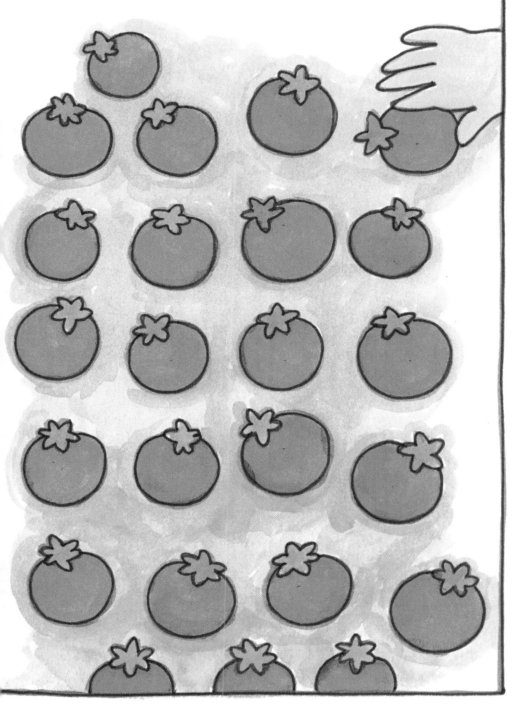

"Strega Nona, Signora Goat
is eating the laundry!"
said Bambolona. "Quick!"

"Oh," said Big Anthony. "Strega Nona did not finish counting her tomatoes."

"I will help her."

"One, two, three . . ."

"Now I can finish with my tomatoes," said Strega Nona.

"Who put
my tomatoes back?"
she asked.

"I did, Strega Nona," said Big Anthony.

"Oh, thank you,
Big Anthony,"
said Strega Nona.
"You are such a good boy."

"Oh well, he was only trying to help. One, two, three . . ."

For Guy, who grows the best tomatoes, and
Mary Ann, who knows exactly what to do with them

SIMON SPOTLIGHT
An imprint of Simon & Schuster Children's Publishing Division
1230 Avenue of the Americas, New York, New York 10020
This Simon Spotlight edition May 2017
Text and illustrations copyright © 2017 by Tomie dePaola
All rights reserved, including the right of reproduction in whole or in part in any form.
SIMON SPOTLIGHT, READY-TO-READ, and colophon are registered trademarks of Simon & Schuster, Inc.
For information about special discounts for bulk purchases, please contact Simon & Schuster Special Sales at
1-866-506-1949 or business@simonandschuster.com.
Manufactured in the United States of America 1023 LAK
6 8 10 9 7
Library of Congress Control Number 2017932248
ISBN 978-1-4814-8135-9 (hc)
ISBN 978-1-4814-8134-2 (pbk)
ISBN 978-1-4814-8136-6 (eBook)